NABO

COL

LECHUGA

VETERRAGA

To Sandra, and all the people of South America
A. D.

The illustrations in this book are photographs of *arpilleras*
(ar-pee-yair'-ahs) created by members of the Club de Madres
Virgen del Carmen of Lima, Peru.

Arpilleras are wall hangings put together from cut and sewn pieces
of cloth. They were first made in Chile, South America, to tell
stories of important events in day-to-day life. Some arpilleras
even have pockets on the back to hold written parts of the stories.
Arpilleras are now made in Peru, Colombia, and Chile.

Although not all South Americans live like the people in this
story, *Tonight Is Carnaval* tells a little bit about what life is like
for many people in the high Andes Mountains.

TONIGHT IS CARNAVAL

BY ARTHUR DORROS

Illustrated with *arpilleras* sewn by
the Club de Madres Virgen del Carmen of Lima, Peru

DUTTON CHILDREN'S BOOKS   NEW YORK

Wake up, sleepyhead," my mother is calling. But I'm already awake. I'm thinking about Carnaval. This year I will play the *quena,* a flute, with my father in the band. "The quena is the voice of the band—the singer of the band," says Papa. Papa plays with the band every year at Carnaval. People in costumes will parade and dance to the music for three whole days and nights.

Carnaval is in the big village down the valley, and it's only three days away!

"We have a lot of work to do before then," Papa says. We work all year, almost every day, but not during Carnaval!

We get up each day before it is light outside, there is so much to do. Mama takes my little sister, Teresa, to the river to get water. Today Mama washes clothes, too. Papa and I look for firewood to use for cooking. Sometimes we walk a long way to find wood—there are hardly any trees in the high Andes Mountains of South America, where we live.

Today I bring my quena along, so I can practice special songs for Carnaval.

A lot of the songs have a good beat that makes you want to dance. *Tunk tunk, tunk tunk.* Papa's ax chopping a log sounds like the beat of the *bombo,* the drum he will play with the band.

Back home Teresa drops kernels of corn into an empty pot. Mama will boil the corn for our meal. *Pling pling, pling pling pling.* The kernels make sounds like the strings of Uncle Pablo's *charango.* He will play in the band with us too, at Carnaval.

After our meal, we get a field ready for planting. I lead the oxen, to make sure they plow straight. Mama follows us and picks stones out of the loose earth. After Carnaval, my friend Paco and his family will help us plant potatoes. Sometimes Paco's family helps us in our field, and other times we help them in theirs. One of the songs I'm practicing for Carnaval is about working in the fields with friends.

After we plow, I take the hungry llamas high into the mountains to find grass. The best grass is by the crumbling walls of buildings made hundreds of years ago when the Incas ruled these mountains. No one knows how the giant stones were cut to fit together so well. Sometimes we use the old stones to build walls and houses and even terraces for the fields.

I sit on a wall and play my quena. I play a song called *"Mis Llamitas,"* "My Little Llamas," and the llamas leap and dance around. I imagine they are dancing to my music.

The wind whistling across the stones sounds like the windy notes of a *zampoña,* a panpipe. I will play my quena and Paco will play his zampoña when we meet at Carnaval. That's one of the things I like about Carnaval—we get together with friends from our mountain and from all around the valley.

One day is gone. Now we have only today and tomorrow
before tomorrow night—when Carnaval begins. I can hardly wait.
This morning Papa shears wool from an alpaca. An alpaca is like
a llama, but with softer wool. I carry the wool to Mama, so she
can spin it into yarn. "You don't have to run," laughs Mama.
"Carnaval will come as soon as it can."

Mama's fingers twirl the wool round and round. She can spin
yarn while she's walking, or selling vegetables, or doing almost
anything. When she has enough yarn, she'll color it with different
dyes. Grandma will weave it into cloth of many colors. Then
Mama will cut and sew the cloth to make us clothes. Maybe she'll
make me a new jacket.

In the afternoon, we dig potatoes out of the damp earth in a field we planted months ago. The digging usually makes me tired, but today I keep working as fast as I can to help harvest all the potatoes. Tomorrow we'll take them down into the valley to sell at the market. And after the market is cleared away, Carnaval will begin!

We gather red potatoes; yellow, black, and brown potatoes; even purple potatoes. In the Andes, we have hundreds of different kinds of potatoes.

We drop our potatoes into burlap bags, *plonk, plonk, plonk*. The llamas help carry the heavy bags to Antonio's truck. Antonio came from the village today, and he will sleep tonight in his truck.

Finally. Today we take the potatoes to market—then tonight is Carnaval!

I wait and wait to hear the truck start. The motor coughs and groans, *errr errr errr*. But at last Antonio gets it started. Mama, Papa, Teresa, and I—and the potatoes—bounce along in the back of the old truck, which rattles and shakes down the mountain. It stops like a bus to pick up people carrying onions, beans, carrots, turnips, peas, and peppers; llama wool; clothes; and food they have made for Carnaval.

"Hey," I hear someone say, "don't let that chicken eat our corn. We're taking it to market."

The truck bounces over a big bump. I reach down to make sure my quena is not broken. I want people to hear my quena sing when I play at Carnaval.

"Watch out flying over those bumps, Antonio," someone shouts. "Will this old truck fly us to the village?"

"Don't worry," Antonio shouts back. "This old truck and I know how to get there."

People hug when they climb into the truck. We don't see these friends very often. We all stand and look out along the way. People throw water balloons and water from buckets to try to splash us. They're excited about Carnaval.

At the market, I help unload the heavy bags of potatoes, and then I walk around. I love to see the brightly colored piles of vegetables. People trade wool that still smells like llamas or sheep. And the nutty smell of toasted fava beans and corn makes my mouth water.

But today I can't wait until Mama sells all of our potatoes and the market is cleared away. Then people will come out in their costumes. At first it will be hard to see who each person is—many of the people will be wearing masks. I'll find the band. Papa's bombo will start booming, Paco's zampoña will be whistling, and Uncle Pablo's charango plinging. People will start shouting "Play your songs," stamping their feet, swirling, turning, dancing to the music faster and faster because—

TONIGHT IS CARNAVAL.

When I play my quena with the band, people start to sing.
My quena sings and the people sing. I play the special songs I've
learned for Carnaval, about llamas, mountains, and friends.
We play songs with a beat for dancing. Paco and I watch all the
people hold onto each other in one long line that dances—laughing,
winding through the village.

Our band plays under the moon and flickering stars, and we will
play until the sun comes up. We play the songs of our mountain
days and nights...for tonight is Carnaval.

HOW ARPILLERAS ARE MADE

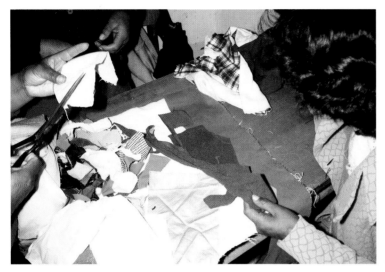

An arpillera-maker draws the design on white cloth. Pieces of cloth are selected and cut to fit the design.

Big pieces of cloth are sewn on to form the background.

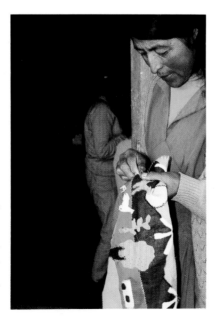

The edges of each shape are neatly stitched, and details are added by sewing on more pieces of cut cloth and by embroidering.

Dolls and other three-dimensional objects (vegetables, musical instruments) are made...

...and sewn onto the arpillera.

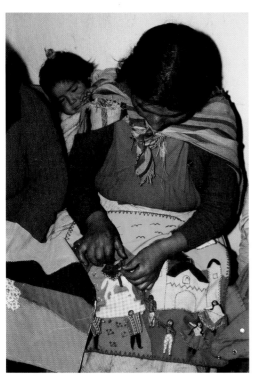

Another arpillera is finished.

Arpillera-makers often work together in groups. These members of the Club de Madres Virgen del Carmen are making vegetables and dolls for arpilleras. With money from the sale of arpilleras, the group also runs a kitchen that helps feed two to three hundred people a day.

GLOSSARY

Quena (kay′-na) A reed flute, held upright and played by blowing into the top. By covering and uncovering the flute's holes with the fingers, the player makes different notes.

Bombo (bom′-bow) A large bass drum carried by the drummer and usually struck with one mallet.

Charango (cha-rahn′-go) A small five-stringed, guitarlike instrument that produces high notes when the strings are plucked.

Zampoña (som-pone′-ya) A panpipe, or flute, made of reeds of different lengths fastened together side by side. Each reed is open at the top and closed at the bottom, and is played by blowing into the top. When blown, each reed gives a different note.

Andes Mountains The cordillera, or range of mountains, in South America that extends from Venezuela and Colombia to southern Argentina and Chile. The Andes are the second highest mountain range in the world.

Carnaval A celebration that takes place just before Lent, the forty weekdays preceding Easter. In the Andes it is celebrated with three days and nights of music (provided by the village band), dancing, and feasting. It is one of the few breaks in the work-filled lives of the people of the Andes.

With thanks to the members of the Comité de Amas de Casa Micaela Bastidas, Cusco, Peru; Gloria Velorio and Proceso Social Cusco; Rosa Malca and Oxfam America; and Christopher Franceschelli, Dutton Children's Books.
   And with special thanks to Maria del Carmen de la Fuente and Allpa and the members of the Club de Madres Virgen del Carmen, Lima, Peru, without whom this project would not have been possible.

Royalties from the sale of this book benefit the vital work of Oxfam America. Additionally, the arpilleras created for this book will be sold by Oxfam America, and all proceeds will go directly to the Club de Madres Virgen del Carmen in Lima, Peru, to support its work in the local community.
   Oxfam America is a nonprofit, international agency that funds self-help development and disaster relief in Africa, Asia, Latin America, and the Caribbean. For further information about Oxfam's programs, or to contribute to Oxfam's efforts, please contact: Oxfam America, 115 Broadway, Boston, MA 02116; (617) 482-1211.

The vegetables shown on the endpapers are, from left to right, carrots, tomatoes, turnips, cabbage, cauliflower, radishes, lettuce, and beets.

Library of Congress Cataloging-in-Publication Data
Dorros, Arthur.
   Tonight is Carnaval/by Arthur Dorros; illustrated with arpilleras sewn by the members of the Club de Madres Virgen del Carmen of Lima, Peru.—1st ed.
       p.   cm.
   Summary: A family in South America eagerly prepares for the excitement of Carnaval.
   ISBN 0-525-44641-9
   [1. Carnaval—South America—Fiction. 2. South America—Fiction.] 1. Title.
PZ7.D7294To 1991   90-32391 CIP AC
[E]–dc20

Published in the United States by Dutton Children's Books, a division of Penguin Books USA Inc.
Designer: Susan Phillips
Printed in Hong Kong
First Edition   10 9 8 7 6 5 4 3

Spanish edition available

ZANAHORIA

TOMATE

COLIFLOR

RABANITO